ROCK

FISH

LITTLE FISH

BOAT

FANCY SNAIL

SLUG SLIME

SNAIL

THEO

SLUG

YARN

BEETLE

NUT

WIGGLY NUT

ELSIE

MOUSE

BERRIES

BIRD

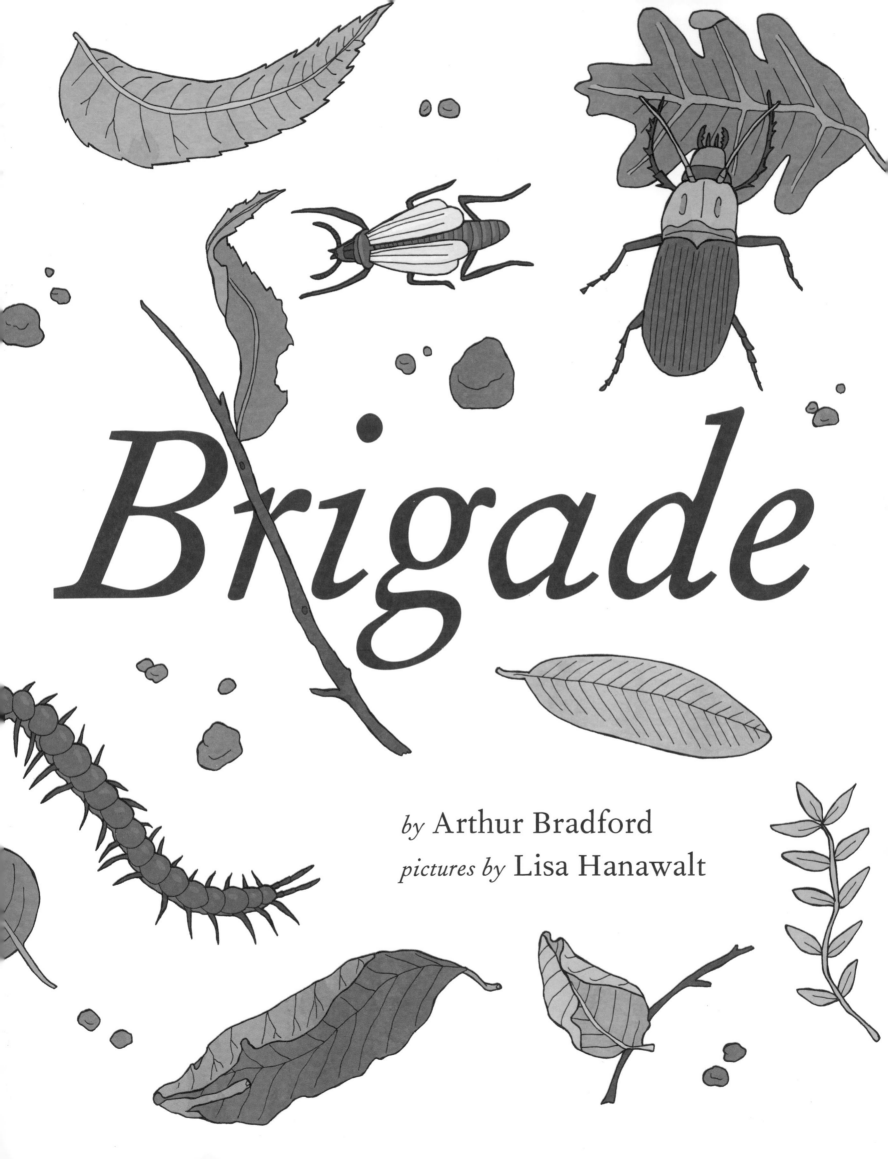

Brigade

by Arthur Bradford

pictures by Lisa Hanawalt

Elsie and Theo were sisters. Elsie was the older sister, but not by much.
Some people thought "Theo" sounded like a boy's name, but Theo always
explained that she was named after her great aunt Theodotia, who was a girl
a very long time ago.

One morning Elsie and Theo were walking to school
when they saw a strange nut wiggling on the ground.

"Why is it wiggling, Elsie?" asked Theo.

"I don't know," said Elsie.

Elsie picked up the nut and watched it bounce up and down on her hand.
Then she held it close to her ear. A tiny voice called out to her from inside.

"Let me out! Please let me out!"

Theo found a small rock, just big enough to crack the
shell, but not so big that it would hurt whoever was inside.

Very carefully, the two girls opened up the wiggling nut.

Out of the broken shell crawled an extremely small walrus.

"Why thank you," said the walrus, brushing himself off. "Thank you very much."

The walrus was so grateful and happy to be out of the nut that he kissed both of the girls upon the backs of their hands. They could feel his tiny whiskers brush against their skin.

"I really don't know how it happened," said the walrus, "but somehow I became stuck inside that nut and I'm quite sure I never would have gotten out if it weren't for you two fine girls."

"I thought walruses were bigger than you," said Elsie.

"Yes, yes, most of them are," said the walrus, "but I am an example of a very small walrus, and there is nothing wrong with that."

"What's your name?" asked Theo.

"I am Benny," said the walrus, "and I am most pleased to meet you."

Theo and Elsie gave Benny some of their lunch because he was hungry after all that time stuck inside the nut. He liked their pretzels best because their salty taste reminded him of the sea from where he had come.

"Would you like to come to school with us?" asked Elsie.

"Why yes, I believe I would," said Benny.

At school, none of the other children believed there was such a thing as a walrus who could fit in someone's pocket, but then Theo pulled Benny out of her pocket and everyone had to admit that they were wrong.

Each of the children wanted to hold Benny but he said, "Please, too much handling is bad for my skin. How about I sing you a song instead?"

So Benny sang them a walrus song which went like this:

> *Oh, to be back in the sea*
> *where a walrus can swim free…*
> *Such a wish is good for fish*
> *but it's also fine for me…*

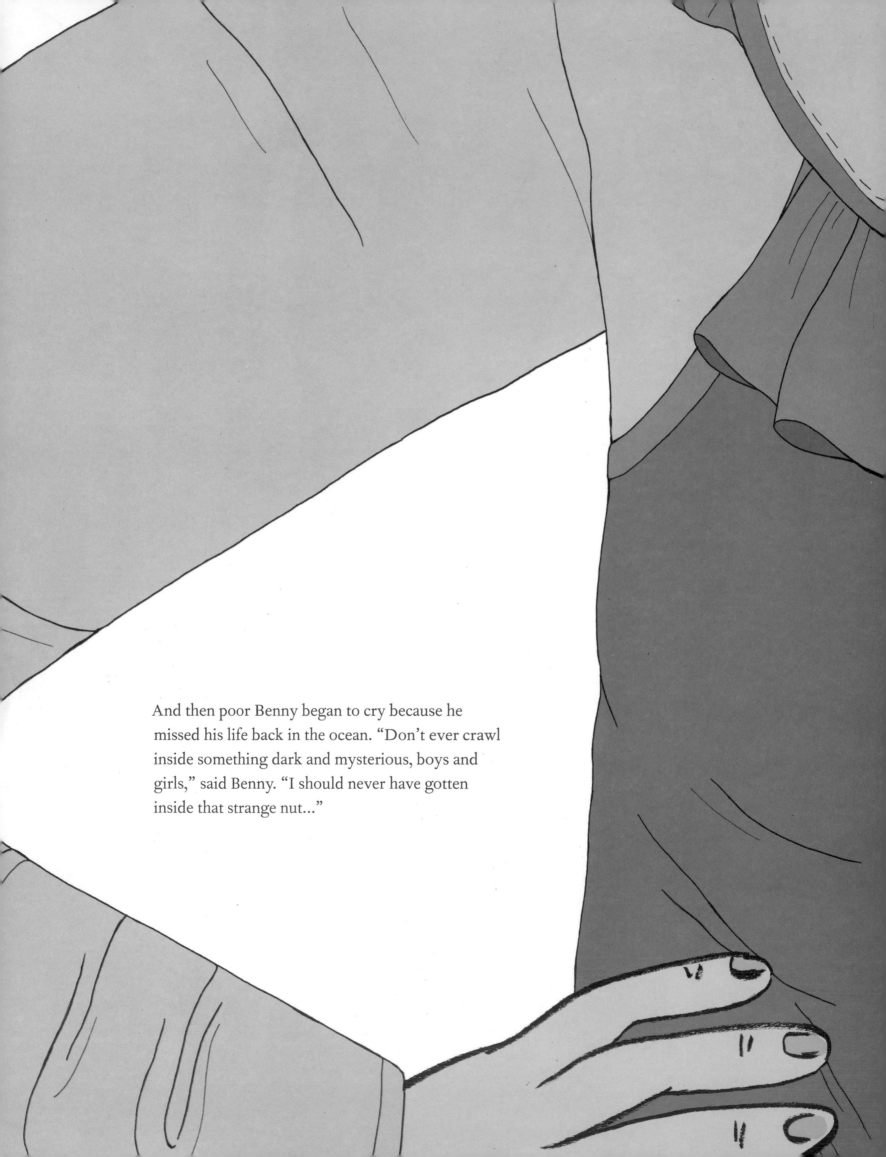

And then poor Benny began to cry because he
missed his life back in the ocean. "Don't ever crawl
inside something dark and mysterious, boys and
girls," said Benny. "I should never have gotten
inside that strange nut..."

The boys and girls all agreed that they would not crawl into dark holes and caves without knowing what lay ahead.

Then they decided to build Benny a boat, a very small one which they could place in the nearby creek. Perhaps that creek would lead to the ocean and Benny could return home.

They built Benny the finest boat any of them
had ever seen. It even had a proper sail, made
from a fresh piece of cloth.

On it, they wrote, "BENNY'S BRIGADE."

"What's a brigade?" asked Benny.

"A brigade is a group of soldiers," said Gus, the boy who'd written the words.

"But I don't have a brigade," said Benny, a little sadly.

And that's when they heard a chorus of tiny voices coming from underneath a log. "We'll be your brigade!" said the voices.

Gus and Elsie lifted up the log and there stood three healthy, fat slugs, ready for adventure.

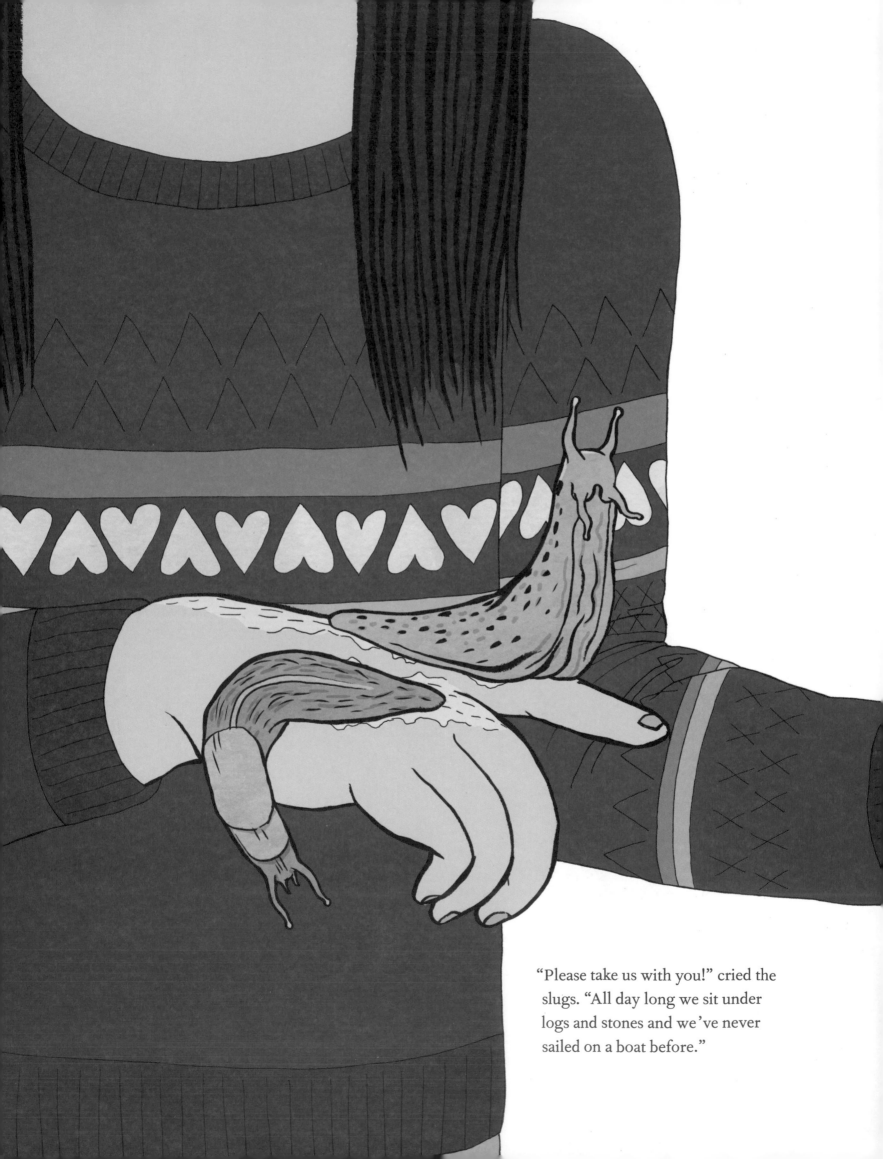

"Please take us with you!" cried the slugs. "All day long we sit under logs and stones and we've never sailed on a boat before."

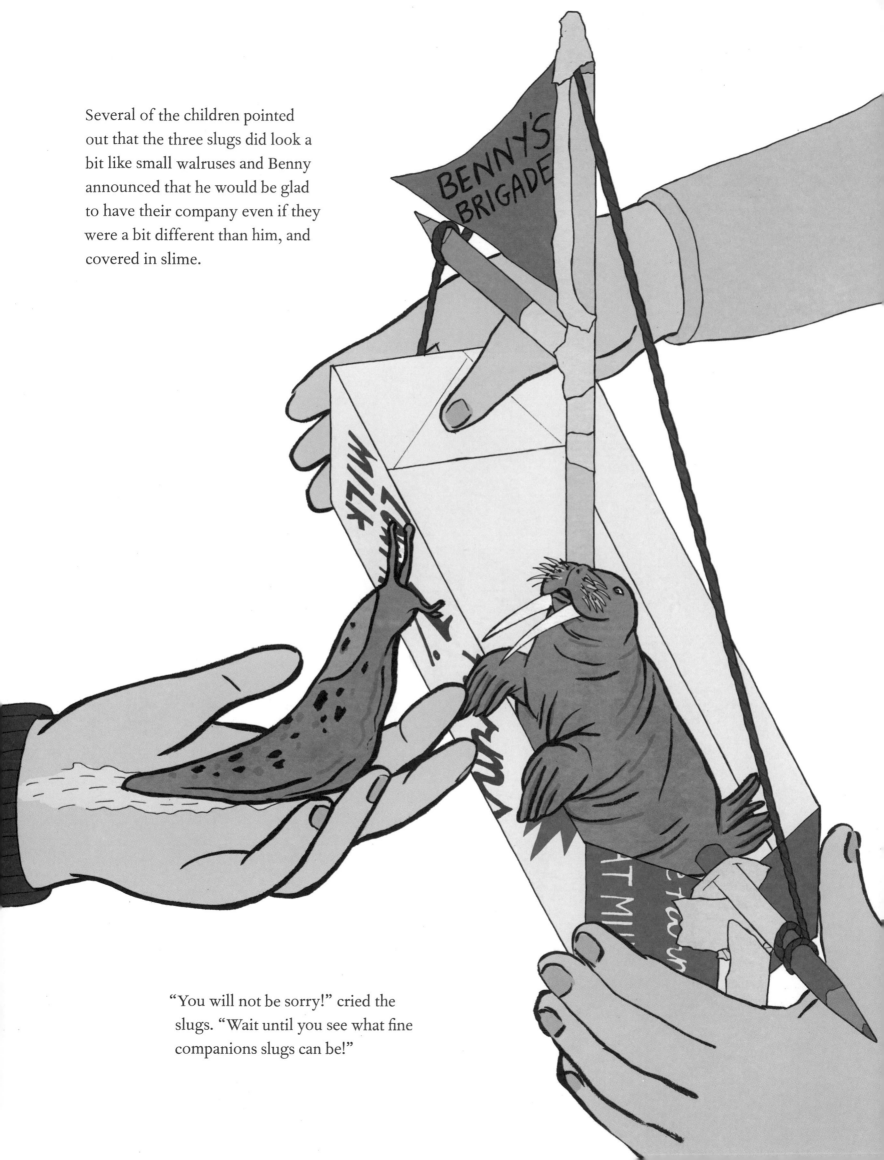

Several of the children pointed out that the three slugs did look a bit like small walruses and Benny announced that he would be glad to have their company even if they were a bit different than him, and covered in slime.

"You will not be sorry!" cried the slugs. "Wait until you see what fine companions slugs can be!"

Then the teacher called the boys and girls inside to begin school.

Quickly Elsie and Theo took the little boat, loaded with its special crew, to the small creek which ran near the playground. They set the boat down and watched it float away.

Some ducks and geese quacked with amazement and Captain Benny shouted to them a warning, "Stay back, you noisy ducks, for we are headed out to sea!"

Before the little boat disappeared around the bend Captain Benny stood up tall on the deck and waved his tiny flipper. "Thank you Elsie and Theo!" he called out, "Thank you, for you have provided us sailors with a fine adventure ahead!"

"You're welcome!" said Elsie and Theo together.

They were sorry to see Benny and the slugs go, but now it was time for school, and they had adventures of their own to which they must attend.

The creek carried Benny's Brigade through a small forest and then under a bridge. It joined up with a stream and then the stream became a large river, wide and deep.

It was there that the three slugs remembered that they would prefer not to travel all the way to the ocean.

"It's not that we don't seek adventure," they told Benny. "It's that the salt water will surely hurt our skin."

"Well, that I can understand," said Captain Benny, for now he also remembered that all slugs detest salt.

Benny looked ahead of him and saw an island sitting in the middle of the river. It was a very small island, perhaps only the size of a truck, or maybe a bus, but it had rocks and dirt and several trees and was plenty big for Benny and his crew.

"We shall steer that way," commanded Captain Benny, "and there we will stay."

"Hooray!" shouted the slugs. "It's the perfect place for the likes of us!"

And this is why you never know what wonderful creatures you might find living on an island, even a very small one, like this.

For Elsie, Theo, and their mother Maggie.
—*Arthur*

Special thanks to Adam Conover, Domitille Collardey, and my Mom and Dad.
This wouldn't have been possible without their support, encouragement, good taste, and honesty.
—*Lisa*

Arthur Bradford is author of the book *Dogwalker* and director of the documentary
film series *How's Your News?*. In the summertime he co-directs Camp Jabberwocky,
one of the nation's longest-running residential camps for people with disabilities.
He lives in Portland, Oregon with his wife and two daughters, Elsie and Theo.

Lisa Hanawalt lives in Brooklyn and was born and raised in Palo Alto, California.
She earned an art degree from UCLA in 2006, she has received multiple awards for
her comic books, and she is pretty good at mimicking the sounds of animals.

Benny's Brigade is Arthur's and Lisa's first book for children.

M^cSWEENEY'S
M^cMULLENS
www.mcsweeneys.net

Printed in Singapore by Tien Wah Press
ISBN: 978-1-936365-61-6
First edition

FISH SANDWICH

FISH BUCKET

TUSK

SHARP-TOOTHED SMILING DOG

ELSIE

STRETCHY DOG

WHISKERS

PRETZEL

BEETLE

PIGTAIL

FLIPPER

VELVET WORM

TOUCAN

TOUCAN'T

ROCK

WILD MINI PIG